AN
STO

Compiled by Julia Eccleshare
Illustrated by Wendy Smith

ORCHARD BOOKS

In the same series:

STORIES FOR BEDTIME
Compiled by Fiona Waters
Illustrated by Penny Dann

For Barnaby
JE
For Jann
WS

ORCHARD BOOKS
96 Leonard Street, London EC2A 4RH
Orchard Books Australia
14 Mars Road, Lane Cove, NSW 2066
ISBN 1 85213 381 3 (hardback)
ISBN 1 85213 664 2 (paperback)
First published in Great Britain 1992
First paperback publication 1994
This selection copyright © Julia Eccleshare 1992
Illustrations copyright © Wendy Smith 1992
The rights of Julia Eccleshare as the compiler and of Wendy Smith
as the illustrator of this work have been asserted by them in
accordance with the Copyright, Designs and Patents Act, 1988.

A CIP catalogue record for this book is available from the British
Library.

Printed in Malaysia

Contents

How the Animals Got Tails

ANNE ENGLISH

There once was a time when none of the animals in the world had tails—not a single one. The horse had no tail to swish away the flies. The dog had no tail to wag when he was happy. And the monkey had no tail to curl round the branches when he was jumping from tree to tree.

The wise lion, who was King of the animals, knew there was something missing, and he thought and thought until he had a clever idea.

"Animals. Animals," he roared, "I, the lion, the King of all the animals, command you to come to a meeting in the Great Meadow. Roar, roar!"

When they heard the lion roar every animal from far and near came hurrying to the Great Meadow. First came the fox and the squirrel, then the horse, the dog and the cat. Then came the monkey and the mouse. The lion waited for them all to arrive. "Sit in a circle round me," he told them, "and hear what I have to say." More and more animals came until the circle was almost complete. The elephant and the pig were nearly late, but last of all was the rabbit. He had been eating a carrot when he heard the lion roar, and had finished it before coming to the Great Meadow. And now he was the very last to arrive.

The lion held up his paw for silence. "Friends," he said, "I have been thinking." He paused. "I have been thinking that something is missing for all of us, so I have invented—TAILS." And he held up a huge bag full of tails.

"You will get one each," he told the animals, "and wear your own always." How the animals clapped and cheered their clever leader. "Now, first come, first served," said the lion, "and as I was here first I get the first tail." And from the bag he pulled a marvellous long golden tail with a black tassel at the end, and put it on himself. How wonderful it made him look. He waved it proudly, while the animals watched, and waited for their tails.

The lion stood in the circle
and called out, "The fox".
He gave the fox a long,
thick bushy tail, like a brush.
Fox put it on
and went away proudly.

"Next, the squirrel," said
the lion. And the squirrel too
got a huge bushy tail, which
he curved up over his back
before leaping away.

The horse came next, and from
the bag the lion pulled a
long, strong, black tail,
combed out until it
was silky and straight.
The horse was delighted,
and galloped off swishing
his new tail from side to side.

The cat and the dog came
into the circle together, and
they each received a straight
tail, which would wave or
wag from side to side, or up
and down, as they pleased.

The monkey was given an extremely long tail. He curled it over his arm, so that he wouldn't trip over it, and went jumping away into the trees.

By now the bag of tails was half empty, so there was not much choice for the elephant when he came in his turn. In fact his tail looked like a piece of chewed string—just look at it, if you see an elephant. But he put it on quite happily, and lumbered off.

"Mouse," called the lion, and the mouse came. Now considering how small a mouse is, he did very well, for the tail pulled from the bag for him was very long indeed. Mouse put it on and scuttled away, trailing his tail behind him.

"Humph!" said the lion, as the pig came up. "Not much left now," and he took out yet another straight stringy tail. The pig was not pleased. "The elephant and the mouse have tails like that," he said. "Can I have

something different, please?" The lion shook his head. "Sorry," he said, "you arrived almost last, and this is all there is." "Oh, very well then," said the pig, taking the stringy tail and looking at it crossly.

"This will just not suit me," he muttered. "Just imagine a pig with a straight tail!" As he walked away he trod on a thick twig. "Hoink, hoink," he grunted, "I have an idea. Lions aren't the only ones with brains."

And he took his tail and wrapped it tightly round the twig. When he pulled the twig out the tail stayed curly. "I like that better," pig said, and he stuck on his new curly tail.

Last of all to receive a tail was the rabbit. By now the lion was rather tired of tails, and he hurriedly shook the bag upside down to get out the last one. It was tiny—just a tiny thin piece of tail. Poor rabbit was disappointed, but

he knew there was nothing else, so he thanked the lion and took the tail. But it was so small he couldn't bring himself to put it on.

"This is just a nothing tail," he told himself. "Not a bushy tail, like the fox's, or swishy like the horse's. Not even long enough to wave or wag. I will look silly with this one." He sighed. The lion had given them all tails, and they would have to wear them, rabbit knew.

As the rabbit wandered along, thinking about his piece of tail, he came to a prickly bush, and *he* had a wonderful idea. "Rabbits can think as well as lions and pigs," he said. And he took his tail and stroked it gently backwards and forwards over the prickles, until the tail became soft and round. "That's better," thought rabbit, looking at it happily. Then he stuck on his new fluffy tail, and bobbed away merrily.

Two Legs or Four?

DICK KING-SMITH

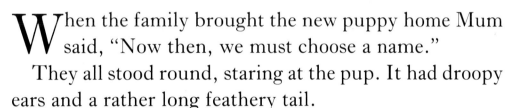

When the family brought the new puppy home Mum said, "Now then, we must choose a name."

They all stood round, staring at the pup. It had droopy ears and a rather long feathery tail.

No one knew quite what sort of dog it was.

"Come on," said Dad. "What shall we call him?"

Mandy, who was six, nearly seven, said, "Jeremy."

"Why Jeremy?"

"After Jeremy Fisher. We read about him in school today."

"But he was a frog, not a dog."

"I'd like to call him Toblerone," said Polly who was five.

"Why Toblerone?"

"Because he's sort of chocolate coloured and that's my favourite."

"The trouble with names like Jeremy and Toblerone is that they're so long," said Dad. "A dog should really have a short name. It's easier for him to learn and for us to say."

"I know!" said Ben. Ben was three.

"What?" they all said.

"We could call him Ben," said Ben.

"But that's your name too!" they all cried.

"I know. But it's short."

"That's silly," said Mandy. "I shall call him Jeremy," and she walked out of the room calling, "Come along, Jeremy." But the puppy took no notice.

Then Polly walked out too calling, "Toblerone, come along, Toblerone." But the puppy still took no notice. It stayed sitting in front of the small boy, wagging its rather long feathery tail. In some ways they were rather alike. Both had brown hair and short legs and were rather fat.

"You try going out of the room, Ben," said Dad.

"And you call the puppy," said Mum.

"And see what happens," they said.

They smiled at one another. Nothing would happen, they thought.

"OK," said Ben. "Come on, Ben," he said, and he trudged out with the puppy following close at his heels.

Mum and Dad looked at one another with their mouths open. In a moment Mandy and Polly came running back into the room. "It's not fair!" they cried. "He's our puppy too. But he's just following Ben round the garden, and he won't take any notice when we call him."

"What did you call?" asked Dad.

"Jeremy," said Mandy.

"Toblerone," said Polly.

"Try saying 'Ben'," said Mum.

So they all went out into the garden, and the two girls called, "Ben!" and the puppy came running.

"See?" said Mum. "He answers to his name."

"It's going to be very confusing," said Dad.

In fact, as time went by, they found it was rather useful to have both a son and a dog with the same name. Because Mandy and Polly were at school, Ben spent all day with Ben, and the same words served for both. "Be quiet, Ben!" for instance, stopped one yelling and the other yapping, and both came when the name was called, and sat down when they were ordered, and each looked equally pleased when told "What a good boy, Ben!"

And indeed Ben was a good boy or rather a good puppy. He never made messes on the carpets, he never chewed curtains or covers, he ate well and he slept soundly at night. As well as learning the ordinary things that dogs learn, he took to copying everything the boy did.

If Ben laughed, Ben barked.

If Ben cried, Ben howled.

If Ben lost his temper and roared angrily, Ben growled.

And one day, would you believe it, Mum looked out of the window to see, not one, but two Bens turning somersaults on the lawn.

Sometimes, of course, there was confusion, like: "*I took*

Ben to have his jabs today."

"To the doctor or the vet?"

Or: *"Ben wants a biscuit."*

"Custard cream or Bonio?"

Or: *"Ben's been ever so good today."*

"Good boy or good dog?"

But mostly it worked very well. Until one day it all changed.

Dad came home to find Mum at her wits' end.

"Thank goodness you're back," she said.

"Why? What's up?"

"Ben has been very naughty," said Mandy.

"He won't do a single thing Mum says," added Polly.

"Which Ben? Two legs or four?"

"Two," said Mum. "I just don't know what's the matter with him."

At that moment Ben the boy came into the room followed by Ben the dog.

"Speak to him," said Mum to Dad.

"Come here, Ben," said Dad.

The dog obeyed.

The boy stayed where he was.

"D'you hear me, Ben?" said Dad.

The boy did not reply.

The dog wagged its rather long feathery tail.

"You see?" said Mum.

Dad went over and squatted down before his son. "What's the matter? Why don't you answer me?"

"I thought you were talking to the dog. You said 'Come here, Ben' and 'D'you hear me, Ben?'"

"But that's your name too!" they all cried.

"No, it's not," said the small boy.

He stroked the fat brown puppy's hairy coat. "He can keep that name," he said. "I've grown out of it. It's too short for me. I need a new one."

"What d'you want us to call you then?" asked Mum.

"Jeremy?" said Mandy.

"Toblerone?" said Polly.

Their little brother shook his head. "Not long enough," he said.

"Well, let's see," said Dad, laughing. "How about . . . Bartholomew?"

At the sound of this name, the puppy wagged its rather long feathery tail like mad.

The boy grinned all over his face.

"He likes it!" cried his sisters.

"Bartholomew?" cried his mother.

"Yes, Mum?"

The Butterfly Who Sang

TERRY JONES

A butterfly was once sitting on a leaf looking extremely sad.

"What's wrong?" asked a friendly frog.

"Oh," said the butterfly, "nobody really appreciates me," and she parted her beautiful red and blue wings and shut them again.

"What d'you mean?" asked the frog. "I've seen you flying about and thought to myself: that is one hell of a beautiful butterfly! All my friends think you look great, too! You're a real stunner!"

"Oh *that*," replied the butterfly, and she opened her wings again. "Who cares about *looks*? It's my singing that nobody appreciates."

"I've never heard your singing; but if it's anywhere near as good as your looks, you've got it made!" said the frog.

"That's the trouble," replied the butterfly, "people say they can't hear my singing. I suppose it's so refined and so high that their ears aren't sensitive enough to pick it up."

"But I bet it's great all the same!" said the frog.

"It is," said the butterfly. "Would you like me to sing for you?"

"Well . . . I don't suppose my ears are sensitive enough to pick it up, but I'll give it a try!" said the frog.

So the butterfly spread her wings, and opened her mouth. The frog gazed in wonder at the butterfly's beautiful wings, for he'd never been so close to them before.

The butterfly sang on and on, and still the frog gazed at her wings, absolutely captivated, even though he could hear nothing whatsoever of her singing.

Eventually, however, the butterfly stopped, and closed up her wings.

"Beautiful!" said the frog, thinking about the wings.

"Thank you," said the butterfly, thrilled that at last she had found an appreciative listener.

After that, the frog came every day to listen to the butterfly sing, though all the time he was really feasting his eyes on her beautiful wings. And every day, the butterfly tried harder and harder to impress the frog with her singing, even though he could not hear a note of it.

But one day a moth, who was jealous of all the attention the butterfly was getting, took the butterfly on one side and said: "Butterfly, your singing is quite superb."

"Thank you," said the butterfly.

"With just a little more practice," said the cunning moth, "you could be as famous a singer as the nightingale."

"Do you think so?" asked the butterfly, flattered beyond words.

"I certainly do," replied the moth. "Indeed, perhaps you already *do* sing better than the nightingale, only it's difficult to concentrate on your music because your gaudy wings are so distracting."

"Is that right?" said the butterfly.

"I'm afraid so," said the moth. "You notice the nightingale is wiser, and wears only dull brown feathers so as not to distract from her singing."

"You're right!" cried the butterfly. "I was a fool not to have realized that before!" And straight away she found some earth and rubbed it into her wings until they were all grey and half the colours had rubbed off.

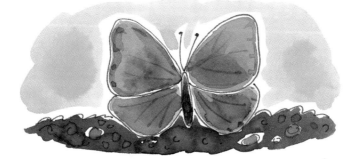

The next day, the frog arrived for the concert as usual, but when the butterfly opened her wings he cried out: "Oh! Butterfly! What have you done to your beautiful wings?" And the Butterfly explained what she had done.

"I think you will find," she said, "that now you will be able to concentrate more on my music."

Well, the poor frog tried, but it was no good, for of course he couldn't hear anything at all. So he soon became bored, and hopped off into the pond. And after that the butterfly never *could* find anyone to listen to her singing.

How the Camel Got His Hump

RUDYARD KIPLING

In the beginning of years, when the world was so new-and-all, and the Animals were just beginning to work for Man, there was a Camel, and he lived in the middle of a Howling Desert because he did not want to work; and besides, he was a Howler himself. So he ate sticks and thorns and tamarisks and milkweed and prickles, most 'scruciating idle: and when anybody spoke to him he said "Humph!" Just "Humph!" and no more.

Presently the Horse came to him on Monday morning, with a saddle on his back and a bit in his mouth, and said, "Camel, O Camel, come out and trot like the rest of us."

"Humph!" said the Camel; and the Horse went away and told the Man.

Presently the Dog came to him, with a stick in his mouth, and said, "Camel, O Camel, come and fetch and carry like the rest of us."

"Humph!" said the Camel; and the Dog went away and told the Man.

Presently the Ox came to him, with the yoke on his neck, and said, "Camel, O Camel, come and plough like the rest of us."

"Humph!" said the Camel; and the Ox went away and told the Man.

At the end of the day the Man called the Horse and the Dog and the Ox together, and said, "Three, O Three, I'm very sorry for you (with the world so new-and-all); but

that Humph-thing in the Desert can't work, or he would have been here by now, so I am going to leave him alone, and you must work double-time to make up for it."

That made the Three very angry (with the world so new-and-all), and they held a palaver, and an *indaba*, and a *punchayet*, and a pow-wow on the edge of the Desert; and the Camel came chewing milkweed *most* 'scruciating idle, and laughed at them. Then he said "Humph!" and went away again.

Presently there came along the Djinn in charge of All Deserts, rolling in a cloud of dust (Djinns always travel that way because it is Magic), and he stopped to palaver and pow-wow with the Three.

"Djinn of All Deserts," said the Horse, "*is* it right for any one to be idle, with the world so new-and-all?"

"Certainly not," said the Djinn.

"Well," said the Horse, "there's a thing in the middle of your Howling Desert (and he's a Howler himself) with a long neck and long legs, and he hasn't done a stroke of work since Monday morning. He won't trot."

"Whew!" said the Djinn, whistling, "that's my Camel, for all the gold in Arabia! What does he say about it?"

"He says 'Humph!'" said the Dog, "and he won't fetch and carry."

"Does he say anything else?"

"Only 'Humph': and he won't plough," said the Ox.

"Very good," said the Djinn. "I'll humph him if you will kindly wait a minute."

The Djinn rolled himself up in his dust-cloak, and took a bearing across the desert, and found the Camel most 'scruciatingly idle, looking at his own reflection in a pool of water.

"My long and bubbling friend," said the Djinn, "what's this I hear of you doing no work, with the world so new-and-all?"

"Humph!" said the Camel.

The Djinn sat down, with his chin in his hand, and began to think a Great Magic, while the Camel looked at his own reflection in the pool of water.

"You've given the Three extra work ever since Monday morning, all on account of your 'scruciating idleness," said the Djinn; and he went on thinking Magics, with his chin in his hand.

"Humph!" said the Camel.

"I shouldn't say that again if I were you," said the Djinn; "you might say it once too often. Bubbles, I want you to work."

And the Camel said "Humph!" again; but no sooner had he said it than he saw his back, that he was so proud of, puffing up and puffing up into a great big lolloping humph.

"Do you see that!" said the Djinn. "That's your very own humph that you've brought upon your very own self by not working. Today is Thursday, and you've done no work since Monday, when the work began. Now you are going to work."

"How can I," said the Camel, "with this humph on my back?"

"That's made a-purpose," said the Djinn, "all because you missed those three days. You will be able to work now for three days without eating, because you can live on your humph: and don't you ever say I never did anything for you. Come out of the Desert and go to the Tree, and behave. Humph yourself!"

And the Camel humphed himself, humph and all, and went away to join the Three. And from that day to this the Camel always wears a humph (we call it "hump" now, not to hurt his feelings); but he has never yet caught up with the three days that he missed at the beginning of the world, and he has never yet learned how to behave.

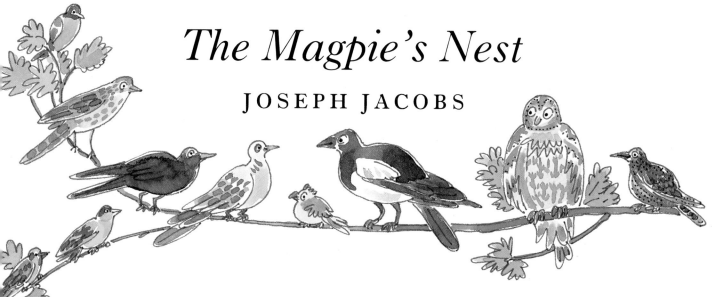

The Magpie's Nest

JOSEPH JACOBS

Once upon a time, all the birds of the air came to the magpie and asked her to teach them how to build nests. For the magpie is the cleverest bird of all at building nests. So she put all the birds round her and began to show them how to do it. First of all she took some mud and made a sort of round cake with it.

"Oh, that's how it's done," said the thrush; and away it flew, and so that's how thrushes build their nests.

Then the magpie took some twigs and arranged them round in the mud.

"Now I know all about it," says the blackbird, and off he flew; and that's how the blackbirds make their nests to this very day.

Then the magpie put another layer of mud over the twigs.

"Oh, that's quite obvious," said the wise owl, and away it flew; and owls have never made better nests since.

After this the magpie took some twigs and twined them round the outside.

"The very thing!" said the sparrow, and off he went; so sparrows make rather slovenly nests to this day.

Well, then the magpie took some feathers and stuff and lined the nest very comfortably with it.

"That suits me," cried the starling, and off it flew; and very comfortable nests have starlings.

So it went on, every bird taking away some knowledge of how to build nests, but none of them waiting to the end.

Meanwhile the magpie went on working and working without looking up till the only bird that remained was the turtle-dove, and that hadn't paid any attention all along, but only kept on saying its silly cry: "Take two, Taffy, take two-o-o-o."

At last the magpie heard this just as she was putting a twig across. So she said: "One's enough."

But the turtle-dove kept on saying: "Take two, Taffy, take two-o-o-o."

Then the magpie got angry and said: "One's enough, I tell you."

Still the turtle-dove cried: "Take two, Taffy, take two-o-o-o."

At last, and at last, the magpie looked up and saw nobody near her but the silly turtle-dove, and then she got extremely angry and flew away and refused to tell the birds how to build nests again. And that is why different birds build their nests differently.

Terrible Tiger's Party

ANITA HEWETT

"A tea party, that's what I'll have," said Tiger. "Not an A party, or a B party, or a C party, but a T party. So all the things at my party must be T things, like tart, and toffee, and tapioca."

Terrible Tiger went to a teak tree. He sat on the ground. His great voice roared, "Come to my T party. Come to the teak tree, Tree-mouse, Toddy Cat, and Two-horned Rhinoceros. Come to my T party."

They came to the party but they forgot to bring a present.

Tiger lifted his great yellow head and his rough voice roared out over the jungle, "Where is my present, my T party present? Where is my T present?"

Tree-mouse, Toddy Cat and Two-horned Rhinoceros stood in a row and looked at their feet. Then they said,

"We forgot it. We're dreadfully sorry. Would a turtle-top suit you, or a tree-pie bird, or perhaps a tin of treacle for a very special treat?"

"No," roared Tiger. "Bring me a tiger lily."

Mouse said, "I beg your pardon, Mr Tiger, but there is no such thing. There is not a mouse lily."

Cat said, "There is not a cat lily."

Rhinoceros said, "There is not a rhinoceros lily. So why should there be a tiger lily?"

"Because I say there *is*," roared Tiger. "Get me a tiger lily. Get it, I tell you."

Tree-mouse, Toddy Cat, and Two-horned Rhinoceros searched in the swamp and they searched in the rice fields. But they could not find a tiger lily.

"I'm tired," said Tree-mouse. "Take him a turtle-top."

So back they went to the teak tree, and said: "We're sorry, Mr Tiger, we couldn't find the tiger lily. We've brought you back a turtle-top to shade you from the sun."

Terrible Tiger swished his tail.

"It isn't a turtle-top at all," he growled. "It's a shell, I tell you. Get me a tiger lily."

Tree-mouse, Toddy Cat, and Two-horned Rhinoceros searched among the mango trees and they searched among the sheeshum trees. But they could not find the tiger lily.

"What's the use of trying any longer?" said Toddy Cat. "Take old Tiger a tree-pie bird."

So back they went to the teak tree and said, "We're sorry, Mr Tiger, the lily wasn't there. So we've brought you back a tree-pie to sing you a song."

Terrible Tiger showed his teeth.

"It isn't a tree-pie at all," he growled. "It's a bird I tell you. Get me a tiger lily."

Tree-mouse, Toddy Cat, and Two-horned Rhinoceros looked beneath the magnolia flowers and they looked beneath the rhododendrons, but they could not find the tiger lily.

"It's just a lot of trouble for nothing," said Rhinoceros. "Take old Tiger some honey from the bees. I know he likes it. I've seen him eating it, and licking his lips, and smiling to himself."

"Honey's not a T thing," Toddy Cat said. "Terrible Tiger is having a T party. Honey is an H thing. It won't do at all."

"Bother old Terrible Tiger," said Rhinoceros. "We'll tell him it's treacle. He'll never know the difference."

They found a tin and filled it with honey. Then back to the teak tree they went and said, "We're sorry, Mr Tiger, we couldn't find the lily, so we've brought you back some treacle for a very special treat."

Terrible Tiger lost his temper. He snarled and he roared and he gnashed his teeth. Tree-mouse, Toddy Cat, and Two-horned Rhinoceros said, "What a fuss!" and they ran away to hide. They sat on the grass behind a rhododendron bush.

Tiger thought they had gone for ever.

He stopped roaring, and smiled to himself.

He took one tiny taste of the honey.

"It's delicious," he said. "I like it. I shall eat it."

He pushed his bristly face in the tin, and licked and licked till his ears and nose and whiskers were sticky all over with the sweet, yellow honey.

And because his face was in the tin, he did not see the stinging bees that came buzzing into the teak tree branches.

Buzz came the first bee.

Buzz came the second bee.

Buzz buzz buzz came a hundred busy stinging bees.

When Tiger had emptied the honey tin he yawned.

"Delicious!" he said. "And now I'll go to sleep."

The bees looked down at the sweet yellow honey that was sticking to his ears and his nose and his whiskers.

Buzz came the first bee.

Buzz came the second bee.

Buzz buzz buzz came a hundred busy stinging bees.

They sat on Terrible Tiger's head, and licked at the honey on his bristly face.

Terrible Tiger swished his tail. He snarled and he roared and he lost his temper. He banged at the bees with his paw, and shouted, "Stop it! I'm Terrible Tiger, I tell you. Stop it! Stop it at once, I tell you."

The bees were exceedingly cross with Tiger. They stung him on his ears and his bristly face. Terrible Tiger sprang in the air. He ran through the jungle roaring with rage, and the stinging bees chased him, buzzing round his head.

Tree-mouse, Toddy Cat, and Two-horned Rhinoceros came from behind the bush to watch.

"Look," they said. "Look at the bees. Terrible Tiger was tired of his T party, even before he really began it. He's found something better. Look at the bees. Terrible Tiger is having a B party."

They watched until Tiger had disappeared. Then they went to the teak tree and sat down beneath it. The turtle-top shaded their eyes from the sun, and the tree-pie bird sat on a branch, and sang.

"Now we can have our party," they said. "But we can't have a T party. Where are the T things?"

Tree-mouse said, "*I* shall eat buds."

Toddy Cat said, "*I* shall eat fruit."

Rhinoceros said, "*I* shall eat grass."

"Good!" they said. "We're having an I party. Poor old Tiger. Perhaps he'd like to come."

But where was Tiger? No one knew.

"I don't know. I don't know. I don't know," they said together.

And where was the tiger lily?

I don't know.

The Cat and the Mouse

JAMES REEVES

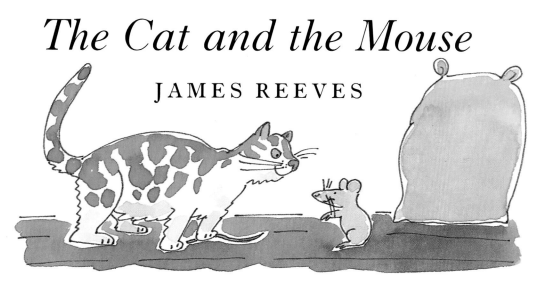

The cat and the mouse played in the malthouse. The cat bit the mouse's tail off. "Pray, puss, give me my tail."

"No," says the cat, "I'll not give you your tail, till you go to the cow, and fetch me some milk."

First she leaped, and then she ran, till she came to the cow, and thus began:

"Pray, Cow, give me milk, that I may give cat milk, that cat may give me my own tail again."

"No," says the cow, "I will give you no milk, till you go to the farmer and get me some hay."

First she leaped, and then she ran, till she came to the farmer, and thus began:

"Pray, Farmer, give me hay, that I may give cow hay, that cow may give me milk, that I may give cat milk, that cat may give me my own tail again."

"No," says the farmer, "I'll give you no hay, till you go to the butcher and fetch me some meat."

First she leaped, and then she ran, till she came to the butcher, and thus began:

"Pray, Butcher, give me meat, that I may give farmer

meat, that farmer may give me
hay, that I may give cow
hay, that cow may give me milk,
that I may give cat milk,
that cat may give me my
own tail again."

"No," says the butcher,
"I'll give you no meat, till you
go to the baker and fetch
me some bread."

First she leaped, and then
she ran, till she came to the
baker, and thus began:

"Pray, Baker, give me bread, that I may give butcher
bread, that butcher may
give me meat, that I may give
farmer meat, that farmer may
give me hay, that I may give
cow hay, that cow may give
me milk, that I may give cat
milk, that cat may give me
my own tail again."

"Yes," says the baker, "I'll
give you some bread,
but if you eat my meal,
I'll cut off your head."

Then the baker gave mouse bread,

and mouse gave butcher bread,

and butcher gave mouse meat,

and mouse gave farmer meat,

and farmer gave mouse hay,

and mouse gave cow hay,

and cow gave mouse milk, and mouse gave cat milk,

and cat gave mouse her own tail again!

The Sparrows' Tug-of-War

STEPHEN CORRIN

One summer morning Mother Sparrow was sitting on her nest full of eggs, enjoying the bright summer sunshine. She could hear the other birds chirping merrily away among the trees and the monkeys chattering for all their worth. In fact everything would have been perfect but for one thing—Father Sparrow was cross, very cross.

"It's that ugly old crocodile," he grumbled. "I went down to bathe in that nice shallow part of the river, you know, and there he was, spread out all over the place. No room for me at all! And when I very politely told him off, he opened his big mouth and laughed. And do you know what he said? 'Go away,' he said, 'I shall stay here as long as I please. Go and have your dip somewhere else.'"

Just as Father Sparrow was speaking, there was a sudden tremendous bump against the tree which tipped him off his twig and very nearly flung Mother Sparrow out of her nest. Father Sparrow flew up to see who it was. It was none other than Brother Elephant taking his morning constitutional. "Hey there, Brother Elephant," called out Father Sparrow with a furious chirrup, "d'you realize that you've nearly shaken my missus out of her nest?"

"Well, what of that, there's no harm done," answered Brother Elephant, without even apologizing.

"No harm done indeed! You've given her the shock of her life. I warn you, Brother Elephant, if you ever do that again, *I'll tie you up*!"

Brother Elephant gave a mighty guffaw. "Ho! Ho! Ho! Tie me up indeed! Go ahead, Father Sparrow. You and all the other sparrows. You are perfectly welcome to tie me up. *But you won't keep me tied*. Neither you nor all the sparrows in the whole wide world." And off he stamped, still guffawing.

"We'll see about that," twittered Father Sparrow, his feathers all a-fluff. Still furiously angry, he flew down to the river where he found the crocodile still all a-sprawl, sunning himself in the nice shallow part of the river.

"I give you warning, Crocodile," chirped Father Sparrow sternly (whereupon the crocodile lazily opened one eye), "that if you are not out of this place by tomorrow morning, *I shall tie you up*."

"Tie me up as much as you like," answered the crocodile closing his eye, "and welcome to it. *But you can't keep me tied*—neither you nor all the sparrows in the whole wide world."

"We'll see about that," said Father Sparrow and whisking his tail he flew back to Mother Sparrow.

All the rest of the day he was very busy discussing matters with all the other sparrows in the forest. And in the afternoon, several hundreds of them got together and, working very hard, they finally made a long length of creeper, very thick and very stout—as strong as any rope.

Soon Brother Elephant came crashing through the forest and, Doying! came bump against Father Sparrow's tree.

"And now what are you going to do, Father Sparrow?" asked Brother Elephant. "Ready to tie me up, eh?"

"Yes, we are," replied Father Sparrow. And he and all his friends flew up and round and round and down and up

again with the long creeper-rope between their beaks, till it was all tightly bound round Brother Elephant's enormous body.

"Now listen to me, Brother Elephant," said Father Sparrow, "when I give the word 'PULL', pull as hard as you can."

"Rightee-ho," answered Brother Elephant, guffawing and shaking with laughter.

But all the sparrows had flown away with the other end of the creeper-rope, pulling it through bush and tree, till they came to the river where Crocodile was.

"So you've come to tie me up, Father Sparrow?" he asked, opening a lazy eye.

"Yes, that's exactly what we *are* going to do," came the reply.

"Tie away," said Crocodile and the sparrows set to work pecking and tugging, flying up and down and up and down again and again and round and round, till the rope was tight and firm round Crocodile's long, slimy body.

"Now," said Father Sparrow, "when I say 'PULL', don't forget, *pull*."

"Right," said Crocodile, half asleep, and the sparrows whisked their tails and flew off.

Then Father Sparrow perched himself in the middle of the creeper-rope where neither Brother Elephant nor Crocodile could see him (and neither of *them* could see the other), and then, in a very loud chirp, he called "PULL".

You can well imagine Crocodile's surprise when he found himself jerked out of his sleep and halfway up the river bank. You can also imagine Brother Elephant's astonishment when, a couple of seconds later, *he* found

himself pulled off his feet—by Crocodile tugging back. Of course, they both thought it was Father Sparrow who was pulling them.

"What a mighty sparrow!" thought Brother Elephant.

"That little bird certainly knows how to pull!" thought Crocodile.

And so now the tug-of-war began in earnest. They each pulled with all their might and main. Sometimes Brother Elephant would gain the upper hand for a few minutes and Crocodile would be dragged up the river bank. Sometimes Crocodile would pull more strongly and Brother Elephant would have to dig his big feet into the earth to stop himself being pulled over. The contest was pretty even, and it went on and on with both of them puffing and panting and groaning, and all the sparrows watching from up above twittered and laughed and enjoyed themselves hugely.

Towards evening, when the sun was beginning to set, Crocodile said to himself, "I'd better not let the other animals see me in this state when they come down to drink at the river." So he called out: "Oh, please, Father Sparrow, please stop tugging and untie me. I promise never to take your bathing place again."

And Brother Elephant cried out in a tiny trumpet: "Father Sparrow, if you stop pulling and untie me, I promise I will never bump into your tree again."

"Oh, very well," said Father Sparrow, "very well."

And so all the sparrows set to work again, hopping and pulling and pecking and chattering, until they had untied Crocodile, who then slid, shamefaced, into the river among the tall reeds and hid himself until it was pitch dark. Then they went and did the same thing to Brother Elephant who then trod quietly away (almost on tip-toe!), thoroughly ashamed of being beaten by such a tiny bird. And all the sparrows, satisfied with their day's work, whisked their tails and flew away.

And Father Sparrow was now able to live in peace and take his dip in his favourite shallow part of the river. And Mother Sparrow was able to sit quietly on her nest of eggs.

Frog and Toad
Go for a Swim

ARNOLD LOBEL

Toad and Frog went down to the river.

"What a day for a swim," said Frog.

"Yes," said Toad. "I'll go behind these rocks and put on my bathing suit."

"I don't wear a bathing suit," said Frog.

"Well, I do," said Toad. "After I put on my bathing suit, you must not look at me until I get into the water."

"Why not?" asked Frog.

"Because I look funny in my bathing suit. That is why," said Toad.

Frog closed his eyes when Toad came out from behind the rocks. Toad was wearing his bathing suit. "Don't peep," he said.

Frog and Toad jumped into the water. They swam all afternoon. Frog swam fast and made big splashes. Toad swam slowly and made smaller splashes.

A tortoise came along the riverbank.

"Frog, tell that tortoise to go away," said Toad. "I don't want him to see me in my bathing suit when I come out of the river."

Frog swam over to the tortoise. "Tortoise," said Frog, "you will have to go away."

"Why should I?" asked the tortoise.

"Because Toad thinks that he looks funny in his bathing suit, and he does not want you to see him," said Frog.

Some lizards were sitting nearby. "Does Toad really look funny in his bathing suit?" they asked.

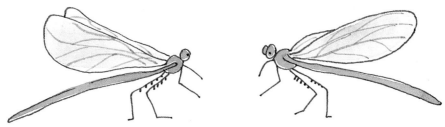

A snake crawled out of the grass. "If Toad looks funny in his bathing suit," said the snake, "then I, for one, want to see him."

"We want to see him too," said two dragonflies.

"Me too," said a field mouse. "I have not seen anything funny for a long time."

Frog swam back to Toad. "I'm sorry, Toad," he said. "Everyone wants to see how you will look."

"Then I'll stay right here until they go away," said Toad.

The tortoise and the lizards and the snake and the dragonflies and the field mouse all sat on the riverbank. They waited for Toad to come out of the water.

"Please," cried Frog, "please go away!"

But no one went away.

Toad was getting colder and colder. He was beginning to shiver and sneeze. "I will have to come out of the water," said Toad. "I am catching a cold."

Toad climbed out of the river. The water dripped out of his bathing suit and down onto his feet.

The tortoise laughed.
The lizards laughed.
The snake laughed.
The field mouse laughed, and Frog laughed.

"What are you laughing at, Frog?" said Toad.

"I'm laughing at you, Toad," said Frog, "because you *do* look funny in your bathing suit."

"Of course I do," said Toad. Then he picked up his clothes and went home.

The Little Half-Chick

KATHLEEN LINES

There was once upon a time a Spanish Hen who hatched out a brood of chickens. She was proud of them for they were plump and handsome children—that is all except one; for when the last shell broke only half a chicken came out! He had one leg, one wing and one eye; he was just a little Half-Chick!

The Hen did not know what in the world to do with the queer little fellow. She tried to keep him near her to protect him from harm. But he soon became bold and headstrong. He went off on his own and pretended not to hear when his mother called him. He had a roving spirit in spite of his one leg, and with a funny little hoppity-kick he could get about very quickly.

As he grew older the little Half-Chick became more and more obstinate and disobedient; and he was rude to his mother and disagreeable to his brothers and sisters.

Then the day came when the little Half-Chick said, "Mother, I'm tired of this old farmyard, I am going off to Madrid to see the King."

His poor mother tried to stop him from being so foolish, but he would not listen. He laughed rudely at her fears and said, "This life is too dull for me. I'm off to see the King." And away he went, hoppity-kick, hoppity-kick, down the high road that led to Madrid.

When he had gone some distance, the little Half-Chick took a short cut through a field, and came to a stream that was clogged with weeds and sticks so that it could not flow freely.

"Little Half-Chick," called the stream. "I can hardly move. Do come and help me by clearing away these sticks and weeds."

"Help you, indeed!" said the little Half-Chick. "I cannot waste my time on you; I'm off to Madrid to see the King." And hoppity-kick, hoppity-kick, away went the little Half-Chick.

A little farther on, the little Half-Chick came to a fire, which was smothered in damp sticks and would soon go out.

"Oh, little Half-Chick," said the fire, "you are just in time to save me. I am almost dead for lack of air. Fan me with your wing, I beg, and put some dry sticks on me."

"Save you, indeed!" said the little Half-Chick. "I have better things to do; I'm off to Madrid to see the King." And hoppity-kick, hoppity-kick, off went the little Half-Chick.

When he had gone a long way, and was on the road near to Madrid, he came to a clump of bushes where the wind was caught and held fast.

"Little Half-Chick," whispered the wind, "do help me to get free from these branches."

"Ho! the very idea!" said the little Half-Chick, "I have no time to waste on you. I am on my way to Madrid to see the King." And hoppity-kick, hoppity-kick, off went the little Half-Chick, in high spirits now, for he could see the roof-tops and towers of Madrid.

Soon he entered the town. He found his way to the King's palace, which he recognized because sentries were keeping guard at the gates. The little Half-Chick went in at the gate, and hoppity-kick, hoppity-kick, he crossed the courtyard on his way to the great front door. But, as he passed the window of the kitchen, the cook looked out and saw him.

"The very thing for the King's dinner!" he said. "I will make some chicken broth." And he picked up the little Half-Chick by his wing, and threw him into the soup pot which hung on the fire.

The water came over the little Half-Chick's feathers, over his head and into his eye. The little Half-Chick cried out, "Water, don't drown me! Don't come so high!"

But the water said, "Little Half-Chick, little Half-Chick, when I was in trouble you would not help me." And the water came higher than ever.

Then the fire blazed up, and burned fiercely. The little Half-Chick cried out, "Fire, don't burn so fiercely! You are scorching me!" But the fire said:

"Little Half-Chick, little Half-Chick, when I was in trouble you would not help me." And the fire burned hotter than ever.

'Fraidy Mouse

ANNE WELLINGTON

Once upon a time there were three grey mice, and they lived in a corner of a barn.

Two of the mice weren't afraid of anything, except the brown tabby cat who lived in the farmhouse. Two of the mice said, "Hi! Look at us. We're tricky and we're quicky and we're fighty and we're bitey. We're not afraid of anything, except the tabby cat."

But the third little mouse said, "Don't look at me. I'm afraid of everything. I'm a 'Fraidy Mouse."

'Fraidy Mouse's brother said, "Don't be ridiculous. There's nothing to be frightened of, except the tabby cat."

'Fraidy Mouse shivered. "I've never seen a tabby cat. Does Tabby Cat stamp with his feet? Does he growl?"

'Fraidy Mouse's brothers said, "Don't be absurd. Tabby Cat sits by the door of the barn.

He sits on the ground
He's big and he's round.
He doesn't move a muscle
Till he hears a little rustle.
Then he'll jump. Thump!
And he'll eat you till you're dead."

Then 'Fraidy Mouse's brothers said, "But Tabby Cat's indoors now. So off we go together to be bold, brave mice."

'Fraidy Mouse was left alone, sitting in the barn. In case he should see something fearsome and frightening, he closed his eyes tightly and fell fast asleep.

While 'Fraidy Mouse was sleeping, the farmer passed the barn. He was carrying a sack full of big brown potatoes. One of the potatoes fell out and rolled to the door of the barn. And there it stayed.

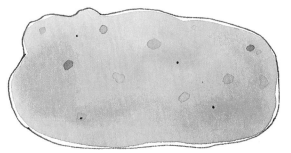

'Fraidy Mouse woke up. He saw that big potato. "Mercy me! It's Tabby Cat, sitting by the door!

He's sitting on the ground,
And he's big and he's round.
He won't move a muscle
Till he hears a little rustle.
Then he'll jump. Thump!
And he'll eat me till I'm dead."

'Fraidy Mouse kept so still that all his bones were aching. Then his brother came back, and they said, "Hi, 'Fraidy Mouse!"

'Fraidy Mouse whispered, "Hush! Oh hush! Don't you see the tabby cat sitting by the door?"

'Fraidy Mouse's brothers said, "Don't be idiotic. That's not a tabby cat. That's a big potato." And they laughed.

'Fraidy Mouse's brothers rolled around laughing, until they were exhausted and had to go to sleep.

But poor little 'Fraidy Mouse cried himself to sleep.

While the mice were sleeping, the farmer passed the barn. He picked the potato up and carried it away. 'Fraidy Mouse twitched in his sleep — dreaming. He dreamed he was a tricky, quicky little mouse.

As the sun went down, the big brown tabby cat came padding up to the barn. And he sat by the door. 'Fraidy Mouse twitched in his sleep again — dreaming. He dreamed he was a fighty, bitey little mouse.

After a while, the mice woke up. The first thing they saw in the twilight was the cat, a big round brown thing sitting by the door. 'Fraidy Mouse's brothers hid away in holes. They stared out with frightened eyes, too terrified to speak.

'Fraidy Mouse thought they were teasing him again, pretending to be frightened of a big brown potato. He wouldn't get caught like *that* again!

He called out, "Hi there! You silly old potato!" The tabby cat was so surprised he didn't move a muscle. 'Fraidy Mouse called again, "I'm only small and 'Fraidy. But I'm not afraid of *you*, you silly old potato. And neither are my tricky, quicky, fighty, bitey brothers."

Tabby Cat said to himself, "What a mouse! If that's a little 'Fraidy Mouse, the smallest, most afraid mouse, his brothers must be terrible. I shan't come here again."

Then Tabby Cat stalked away, pretending not to hurry. And 'Fraidy Mouse said, "Funny! That potato's got a tail!"

'Fraidy Mouse's tricky, quicky, fightey, bitey brothers came creeping from their holes. "Oh, 'Fraidy Mouse!" they said. "How brave you were to talk to the tabby cat like that!"

'Fraidy Mouse thought, "Tabby Cat! That wasn't a potato. I was talking to a real live tabby cat. Oh my!"

Then his legs gave way, and he fell on his back. And his brothers said, "He's resting. It's tiring being so brave!"

The Elephant's Picnic

RICHARD HUGHES

Elephants are generally clever animals, but there was once an elephant who was very silly; and his great friend was a kangaroo. Now, kangaroos are not often clever animals, and this one certainly was not, so she and the elephant got on very well together.

One day they thought they would like to go off for a picnic by themselves. But they did not know anything about picnics, and had not the faintest idea of what to do to get ready.

"What do you do on a picnic?" the elephant asked a child he knew.

"Oh, we collect wood and make a fire, and then we boil the kettle," said the child.

"What do you boil the kettle for?" said the elephant in surprise.

"Why, for tea, of course," said the child in a snapping sort of way; so the elephant did not like to ask any more questions. But he went and told the kangaroo, and they collected together all the things they thought they would need.

When they got to the place where they were going to have their picnic, the kangaroo said that she would collect the wood because she had got a pouch to carry it back in. A kangaroo's pouch, of course, is very small; so the kangaroo carefully chose the smallest twigs she could find, and only about five or six of those. In fact, it took a lot of hopping to find any sticks small enough to go in her pouch at all; and it was a long time before she came back. But silly though the elephant was, he soon saw those sticks would not be enough for a fire.

"Now *I* will go off and get some wood," he said.

His ideas of getting wood were very different. Instead of taking little twigs he pushed down whole trees with his forehead, and staggered back to the picnic-place with them rolled up in his trunk.

Then the kangaroo struck a match, and they lit a bonfire made of whole trees. The blaze, of course, was enormous, and the fire so hot that for a long time they could not get near it; and it was not until it began to die down a bit that they were able to get near enough to cook anything.

"Now let's boil the kettle," said the elephant. Amongst the things he had brought was a brightly shining copper kettle and a very large black iron saucepan.

The elephant filled the saucepan with water.

"What are you doing that for?" said the kangaroo.

"To boil the kettle in, you silly," said the elephant. So he popped the kettle in the saucepan of water, and put the saucepan on the fire; for he thought that you boil a kettle in the same sort of way you boil an egg, or boil a cabbage! And the kangaroo, of course, did not know any better.

So they boiled and boiled the kettle, and every now and then they prodded it with a stick.

"It doesn't seem to be getting tender," said the elephant sadly, "and I am sure we can't eat it for tea until it does."

So then away he went and got more wood for the fire; and still the saucepan boiled and boiled, and still the kettle remained as hard as ever.

It was getting late now, almost dark.

"I am afraid it won't be ready for tea," said the kangaroo, "I am afraid we shall have to spend the night here. I wish we had got something with us to sleep in."

"Haven't you?" said the elephant. "You mean to say you didn't pack before you came away?"

"No," said the kangaroo. "What should I have packed, anyway?"

"Why, your trunk, of course," said the elephant. "That is what people pack."

"But I haven't got a trunk," said the kangaroo.

"Well, I have," said the elephant, "and I've packed it. Kindly pass the pepper; I want to unpack!"

So then the kangaroo passed the elephant the pepper, and the elephant took a good sniff. Then he gave a most enormous sneeze, and everything he had packed in his trunk shot out of it—toothbrush, spare socks, gym shoes, a comb, a bag of bull's-eyes, his pyjamas, and his suit.

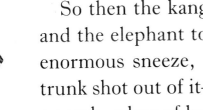

So then the elephant put on his pyjamas and lay down to sleep; but the kangaroo had no pyjamas, and so, of course, she could not possibly sleep.

"All right," she said to the elephant; "you sleep and I will sit up and keep the fire going."

So all night the kangaroo kept the fire blazing brightly and the kettle boiling merrily in the saucepan.

When the next morning came the elephant woke up.

"Now," he said, "let's have our breakfast."

So they took the kettle out of the saucepan; and what do you think? *It was boiled as tender as tender could be!* So they cut it fairly in half and shared it between them, and ate it for their breakfast; and both agreed they had never had so good a breakfast in their lives.

Brer Fox and the Little Rabbits

retold by

MARGARET MAYO

Brer Rabbit's children were good children. They always did what their mother and father told them, from morning till night. When Brer Rabbit said "scoot", they scooted, and when Mrs Rabbit said "scat", they scattered. They did. They were very good children, and if they hadn't been good, there was a time when there wouldn't have been any little rabbits left.

It happened that one day Brer Rabbit was out raiding a cabbage patch, and Mrs Rabbit was visiting some neighbours, so there was nobody in the house but the little rabbits. And while they were playing hide-and-seek, who should walk straight in at the door, but Brer Fox himself.

Soon as the little rabbits saw him, they were afraid, and they sort of huddled close together and watched him.

Now those little rabbits were so fat they made Brer Fox's mouth water, but he was a bit scared of gobbling them up straight off without having some sort of excuse. So he sat down and began to wonder what sort of excuse he was going to make up.

By and by, he saw a great, thick stalk of sugar-cane, standing in a corner, and he cleared his throat and said, "Hey! You young rabbits, go over there and break off a piece of that sweet sugar-cane for me!"

Then the little rabbits went over to the sugar-cane, and they pulled it and they tugged at it. They wrestled with it. But it was no use, they couldn't break it.

Brer Fox hollered at them, loud as he could, "Hurry up there, rabbits! Hurry up! I'm waiting for you!"

The little rabbits hustled around and wrestled with it some more, but they still couldn't break it.

Then, all of a sudden, they heard a little bird singing at the window, and this is the song he sang:

"Use your teeth and gnaw it.
Use your teeth and saw it.
Saw it and gnaw it —
That's how to break it!"

The little rabbits were glad when they heard this, and they got together and sawed and gnawed through the sugar-cane almost before Brer Fox could get his legs uncrossed. Then they brought him a piece of cane. But he didn't eat it. He just sat there trying to think of another excuse for gobbling them up.

By and by, he saw a sieve hanging on the wall, and he stood up and lifted it down. Then he cleared his throat and said, "Come here, you young rabbits! Take this sieve and run down to the spring and fetch me a drink of fresh water."

The little rabbits took the sieve and ran down to the spring and dipped it in the water. But, of course, when they lifted it out, all the water ran through. Then they kept on dipping and lifting, and still the water kept on running through, until at last the little rabbits sat down and began to cry.

And then, all of a sudden, a little bird sitting up in a tree began to sing, and this is the song he sang:

"A sieve holds water the same as a tray,
If you line it with moss and daub it with clay;
Brer Fox gets madder the longer you stay —
So line it with moss and daub it with clay!"

Up jumped the little rabbits and fixed the sieve with moss and clay so that it wouldn't leak. Then they filled it with water and carried it to Brer Fox.

When Brer Fox saw that they had brought the water, he was mighty mad. He pointed at a great, big log and he hollered out, "Little rabbits! Put that log on the fire! And hurry about it!"

Well, they gathered round the log and they tried to lift it. They tried so hard, but it wouldn't budge. Then once again they heard a little bird singing on the roof of the house, and this is the song he sang:

> "*Spit on your hands*
> *And rear back and roll it.*
> *Get right behind it*
> *And push it and roll it.*"

So the little rabbits spat on their hands, and they pushed the log and rolled it along the floor. And just as they got it on the fire, their father, Brer Rabbit himself, came skipping in back from the cabbage patch; and at the same time the little bird flew away.

Then Brer Fox saw that his game was up. He was not going to get a chance to eat those fat little rabbits that day after all. So he stood up and said that it was time for him to go.

"Stay and have something to eat, Brer Fox!" said Brer Rabbit.

But Brer Fox wouldn't stay. He just buttoned up his coat and set off for home, leaving Brer Rabbit and Mrs Rabbit and all the little rabbits to enjoy a great big dinner.

Acknowledgements

The compiler and publishers would like to thank the following for the use of copyright material in this collection.

"The Sparrows' Tug-of-War" © Stephen Corrin 1972, from *A Time to Laugh*, reprinted by permission of Faber and Faber Ltd; "How the Animals Got Tails" © Anne English; "Terrible Tiger's Party" by Anita Hewett, from *The Anita Hewett Animal Story Book*, reprinted by permission of The Bodley Head, Random Century Group; "The Elephant's Picnic" from *The Wonder Dog* by Richard Hughes. Text copyright © 1940 by Harper & Brothers, renewed 1968 by Richard Hughes. Reprinted by permission of David Higham Associates Limited; "The Butterfly Who Sang" © Terry Jones 1981, from *Fairy Tales*, reprinted by permission of Pavilion Books; "Two Legs or Four?" by Dick King-Smith © 1991 by Fox Busters Ltd; "The Half-Chick" © Kathleen Lines 1961; this retelling reprinted by permission of the Kathleen Lines Memorial Fund; "Frog and Toad Go for a Swim" from *Frog and Toad Are Friends* © Arnold Lobel 1970, World's Work Ltd 1971; "Brer Fox and the Little Rabbits" © Margaret Mayo 1991; "The Cat and the Mouse" © James Reeves, from *The Gnome Factory and Other Stories*, Puffin 1986.

Every effort has been made to trace copyright holders, but in a few cases this has proved impossible. The editor and publishers apologise for these unwilling cases of copyright transgression and would like to hear from any copyright holders not acknowledged.